For my sister Sally
who got glasses
M. M.

To my sister Sarah;
also for Libby and Adrian
with love
A. K.

First published in the United States 1992 by
Dial Books for Young Readers
A Division of Penguin Books USA Inc.
375 Hudson Street
New York, New York 10014

Published in Great Britain by All Books for Children
Text copyright © 1991 by Maryann Macdonald
Pictures copyright © 1991 by Anna King
All rights reserved
Printed in Hong Kong
First Edition
1 3 5 7 9 10 8 6 4 2

Library of Congress Cataloging in Publication Data
Macdonald, Maryann.
Little Hippo gets glasses / by Maryann Macdonald.
p. cm.
Summary: Little Hippo is upset when he has to get
glasses until he makes a surprising new friend
who helps him accept his new look.
ISBN 0-8037-0964-1
[1. Hippopotamus—Fiction. 2. Eyeglasses—Fiction.] I. Title.
PZ7.M1486Lj 1992 [E]—dc20 91-11971 CIP AC

Little Hippo Gets Glasses

by Maryann Macdonald · pictures by Anna King

Dial Books for Young Readers New York

"Mama," yelled Howard, "Little Hippo is sitting too close to the television again!"

"Tattletale," whispered Little Hippo.

Mama walked into the room. "Harold, dear," she said, "I think it's time you had your eyes checked."

"My eyes are fine," said Little Hippo.

"We'll see," said Mama.

The next day they went to visit the eye doctor.

"Harold is nearsighted," said the doctor. "He needs glasses for watching television and seeing the blackboard at school."

At school! No one else at school wore glasses. Everyone would make fun of him. And that new pretty hippo, Sophie—she would never, ever talk to him. Not if he wore glasses.

Mama took Little Hippo to buy glasses. He tried
on a pair of red frames. "My!" said the salesman.
"Don't you look handsome!" Little Hippo didn't
think so. He thought he looked silly.

"They're perfect!" said Mama. "Don't you think so, dear?"

To make Mama happy, Little Hippo said yes. But his mind was made up. He was not going to wear glasses to school—no matter what anyone said.

The man placed special glass in the frames. "Now try these on," he said, "and tell me if you can see better." Little Hippo put the glasses on again. Everything looked clearer. He was surprised. But he wasn't going to show it.

"They're OK," Little Hippo said. So the man put the glasses into a neat red case. Mama paid for them and they went home.

In the morning Mama made sure Little Hippo's glasses were packed in his schoolbag. But Little Hippo didn't take them out.

He didn't need them to read his book.
He didn't need them to do his alphabet
or arithmetic.

And he didn't need them to play tag at recess.

But after recess it was time for spelling. Miss Rhinoceros wrote the new words on the board. This is what they looked like to Little Hippo:

Little Hippo looked at Sophie's paper to see
if he could copy from her. But Sophie didn't
have anything written on her paper either.
"What's the first word?" she whispered to him.

At last Sophie had spoken to him! Little Hippo had to answer her. So he reached down into his schoolbag. He took out his glasses. And he put them on. "Elephant," he said. "E-L-E-P-H-A-N-T."

Sophie gave him a funny look. Then she reached down into her schoolbag and took out a pair of glasses. She put them on and smiled at Little Hippo. "Thanks," she said. And she started to copy the spelling words.

Little Hippo copied them too. Everything was
a lot clearer now . . . and Little Hippo didn't feel
silly at all.